The Big Book of
Tricky Riddles for Kids

The Big Book of Tricky Riddles for Kids

400+ RIDDLES!

Corinne Schmitt

Illustrations by Dylan Goldberger

ROCKRIDGE
PRESS

Interior and Cover Designers: Erin Yeung and Linda Snorina
Art Producer: Tom Hood
Editor: Erum Khan
Production Editor: Mia Moran

Illustrations © Dylan Goldberger 2020

ISBN: Print 978-1-64611-263-0 | eBook 978-1-64611-264-7
R0

For Mr. Byer, my fourth grade teacher, who introduced me to the joy of riddles.

Contents

Riddle Me This

Riddles are a fun way to exercise your brain. They're simple questions that require a bit of clever thinking to answer, letting you practice lots of helpful skills like critical thinking, deductive reasoning, attention to detail, creativity, and problem solving. You'll also learn to be patient and persistent, since the answer to a riddle usually isn't obvious.

There are lots of different types of riddles. This book has everything from clever one-liners to challenging brain teasers—and some silly riddles for extra fun. Some answers are on the same page, so you can make a game of it by challenging friends and family. Or you can cover the answers and tackle them yourself!

You may find you have a knack for specific types of riddles, while others take more effort. That's what makes riddles so great! You'll learn some unique ways to think—and have fun doing it.

Let's start riddling!

1

CLEVER QS &
CRAFTY AS

Riddles have been around for thousands of years. The very first recorded riddle is from Mesopotamia in 2350 BCE (find this ancient riddle at the end of the chapter). For centuries, people all over the world have enjoyed trying to stump one another with riddles. Why? Like most other things we do for fun, riddles help distract our minds, and they give us an opportunity to stretch our brains. Just like sports let us practice physical skills, riddles let us practice mental skills. But unlike a game of soccer or basketball, you don't need a large group of people to solve a riddle.

Ready to start having some fun with riddles? This chapter is full of short one-liners with answers that are just as brief. But don't be fooled! You'll find many of these are pretty tricky, so you'll have to think hard—and creatively—to solve them.

1. If you take two apples from three apples, how many do you have?

Two, because that is how many you took. (Told you they're tricky!)

2. How can you stand behind your father while he is standing behind you?

By standing back to back.

3. What has two hands but cannot scratch its face?

A clock.

4. If Sam's parents have three sons and the first two are Huey and Dewey, what is the third son's name?

Sam.

5. In a one-story red house with red walls, red carpet, and red doors, what color are the stairs?

There are no stairs in a one-story house.

6. Which letter comes next in this sequence: M, T, W, T, F, S?

S; the letters are the first letters of each day of the week.

7. If a man stood out in the pouring rain without an umbrella, hat, hood, or canopy over him, but his hair did not get wet, how was it possible?

He's bald.

8. Name two days that start with the letter T besides Tuesday and Thursday.

Today and tomorrow.

9. What kind of room can you eat?

A mushroom.

10. What are two things you can never have for breakfast?

Lunch and dinner.

11. Can a kangaroo jump higher than a mountain?

Of course, because mountains can't jump.

12. Which month of the year has 28 days?

They all do; no month has fewer than 28 days.

13. What can be measured but cannot be seen, taken but not given, and told but not heard?

Time.

14. What five-letter word do even the smartest people pronounce wrong?

The word *wrong*.

15. If two mothers and two daughters go to the store and each buys a new purse, why do they only bring home three purses?

Because there are only three people: a grandmother, her daughter, and her granddaughter.

16. If I have two coins that total 30 cents and one of them is not a quarter, what are the two coins?

A nickel *and* a quarter. If one is not a quarter, the other is!

17. Where does today come before yesterday?

In the dictionary.

18. What has 10 letters and starts with gas?

Automobile.

19. What are some things that can run but not walk?

Water, ink, paint, and noses!

20. When should you give gorilla milk to a baby?

When the baby is a gorilla.

21. How can two babies be born on the same day to the same mother and not be twins?

They are two of the three babies in triplets.

22. How many seconds are in a year?

There are 12: January 2nd, February 2nd, etc.

23. What honorable thing can you break without touching?

A promise.

24. What looks exactly like a cat but isn't a cat?

A picture of a cat or a cat's reflection in a mirror.

25. How can you drop an egg on a concrete floor without cracking it?

Easy—an egg will never crack a concrete floor.

26. A man jumped out of an airplane without a parachute and survived. How?

The plane was on the ground.

27. What food stays hot even if you put it in the refrigerator?

A jalapeño, because it's a hot pepper.

28. How many letters are there in the alphabet? (Hint: The answer is NOT 26!)

There are 11: three in "the" and eight in "alphabet."

MIX IT UP

This is a fun one to stump adults with. See if your family can figure it out without any clues. If they can't get it, let them ask yes-or-no questions to see if that helps.

29. When is it okay to go on red and stop on green?

When eating a watermelon.

30. How do you fix a broken pizza?

With tomato paste.

31. What type of shells do you never find in the ocean?

Dry shells.

32. Name a fruit whose letters can be rearranged to spell another fruit.

Lemon/melon.

33. Which burns longer: white candles or yellow candles?

Neither: candles burn shorter, not longer.

34. What kind of table can you eat?

A vegetable.

35. Which weighs more, a pound of bubble wrap or a pound of bricks?

Neither; they both weigh one pound.

36. What has a bottom at its top?

Legs.

37. Which two words, when put together, have the most letters?

Post office.

SILLY STATS

The US postal service delivers more than 180 million pieces of first-class mail every day! They process more than 5,000 pieces of mail every second.

---

38. What kind of tree can you carry in your hand?

Palm.

39. How do you make the number one disappear?

Add the letter G or N to the beginning so it is gone or none.

40. What three keys cannot open any locks?

Donkey, jockey, and monkey.

41. If you have five grapefruits in your left hand and another five in your right hand, what do you have?

Really big hands.

42. What belongs to you but is used more by other people?

Your name.

43. What can you put in a bag of grain to make it lighter and easier to carry?

A hole.

44. How is it possible to go 30 days without sleeping?

Only sleep at night.

45. Why is it that when something is lost, it's always found in the very last place you looked?

Because after you find it, you stop looking.

46. Why did the little boy stare at the can of juice?

Because it said, "Concentrate."

47. What common verb becomes past tense when you rearrange its letters?

Eat (ate).

48. How can you place a book on the floor so that no one can jump over it?

Lean it against the wall.

49. What do celebrities and air conditioners have in common?

They both have fans.

50. How many birthdays does an 80-year-old woman have?

One . . . everyone has only one *birthday*.

51. What type of band never plays music?

A rubber band.

52. What do you have to break before you can use it?

An egg.

53. Is a $20 bill from 1920 more valuable than a new one?

Yes, $20 is always more than one.

54. Is it ever correct to say, "I is" instead of "I am"?

Yes, when talking about the letter *I*, as in "*I* is the first letter in the word 'is.'"

MIX IT UP

This is another fun one to try on adults. If they answer no, assure them the answer is yes and see if they can come up with an example.

55. How is it that a woman is driving without her headlights on when there is no moon or streetlights, yet she can see a dog in the road ahead?

It is daytime.

56. Where is the ocean deepest?

At the bottom.

57. Name three states that contain no cities or counties.

Solid, liquid, and gas (the three states of matter).

58. What was the longest river in the world before the Amazon River was discovered?

The Amazon River was still the longest, it just had not been discovered yet.

59. Why does Jane, whose birthday is December 25, celebrate her birthday during the summer?

Because she lives in the southern hemisphere, where seasons are the opposite of those in the northern hemisphere.

60. If it takes seven minutes to boil an egg, how long does it take to boil one dozen eggs?

It still only takes seven minutes, since you can boil them all at once.

61. Who always sleeps with shoes on?

A horse.

62. Can the letters in NEW DOOR be rearranged to spell one word?

Yes, ONE WORD uses all the letters from NEW DOOR.

63. What's the name for a person who does not have all their fingers on one hand?

Typical—most people have all ten of their fingers on *two* hands (on one hand they only have half their fingers).

64. What question can you never honestly answer "yes"?

Are you asleep?

65. What four-letter word can be read left to right, even when written upside down or backward?

NOON.

66. What kind of bet can never be won?

An alphabet.

67. What has no hands but is able to build?

A bird.

68. Stupendous is a tricky word. How do you spell it?

I-T.

69. What type of ship is not used to travel in water?

A friendship. Bonus points if you also thought of relationship!

70. Which word does not belong: red, orange, yellow, blue, green, or indigo?

Or.

71. Which is correct: My dog ate the largest half of my sandwich, or my dog ate the larger half of my sandwich?

Neither, because halves are the same size.

72. What is as large as an elephant but weighs nothing at all?

Its shadow.

73. How is it possible to have a room full of people, and yet there isn't a single person there?

Everyone is married.

74. What type of nut has a hole in the center?

A donut.

75. How can you throw a ball as hard as you can and still have it return to you without anyone or anything else touching it?

Throw it straight up in the air.

76. How do you make a line drawn on a piece of paper longer without touching the line?

Draw a shorter line beneath it, and the original line is now the longer of the two.

77. What kind of dress can never be worn?

An address.

78. How many pairs of pants can you put into an empty hamper?

None; as soon as you put anything in, it is not empty anymore.

79. What does a dog have that no other animal has?

Puppies.

80. If Isabella has three daughters and each daughter has a brother, how many children does she have?

Four; three daughters and one son.

81. Noah fell off a 40-foot ladder but did not get hurt. How?

He only fell from the bottom rung.

82. How can a leopard change its spots?

Move from one spot to another.

83. What word is pronounced the same even if you take away four of its letters?

Queue.

84. Will a stone fall faster in a pail of water that is 25 degrees Celsius or in a pail of water that is 25 degrees Fahrenheit?

In the pail of 25 degrees Celsius water since the other pail is frozen.

85. How many legs does an ant have if you call its antennae legs?

Six. Calling its antennae legs does not make them legs.

86. Without needing to know their meanings, what do the words *abstemiously, facetiously,* and *placentious* have in common?

They contain all five vowels in alphabetical order.

> **RIDDLE HISTORY**
>
> *Abstemiously* means that someone eats and drinks in moderation. (They don't overindulge.) *Facetiously* means that what has been said isn't meant to be taken seriously. Long ago, *placentious* was used to refer to a person who is likeable, but the word is no longer commonly used.

87. Why are ghosts such bad liars?

Because you can see right through them.

88. What kind of goose doesn't have feathers?

A mongoose.

89. What kind of ball can be rolled but not bounced or thrown?

An eyeball.

90. Which side of a dog has more fur?

The outside.

91. What two types of cups can you never drink from?

A hiccup and a cupcake.

92. If you throw a blue stone into the Red Sea, what will it become?

Wet.

BRAIN BENDER

93. There is a house. One enters it blind and comes out seeing. What is it? (Note: What is the house?)

A school.

RIDDLE HISTORY

This is the oldest known riddle. It was found engraved on a clay tablet found in ancient Mesopotamia (now Iraq). Kids 4,000 years ago enjoyed riddles as much as we do today!

2

WHAT AM I?

An *enigma* is something mysterious or difficult to figure out. In riddles, the term enigma describes puzzles that have hidden meanings. The questions are asked in a way that is meant to trick you on purpose.

This chapter is full of these kinds of enigmas. Each riddle will provide a brief description, written from the perspective of a specific person, place, or thing, followed by a simple question: "What am I?" They will be more cunning than the one-liners in chapter 1, as each one has been written with the specific goal of fooling you.

Don't worry, they're not too tricky! Try to think of alternative definitions of the words used in the riddles, and use some creative thinking. Once you've done a few, they'll get easier. These riddles are especially fun to figure out with others since different perspectives will help you look at the riddles from several angles.

94. I am weightless, but you can see me. Put me in a jug, and I will make it lighter. What am I?

A hole.

95. I am never quite what I appear to be. I seem simple, but only the wise understand me. What am I?

A riddle!

> **MIX IT UP**
>
> What other clues can you think of for "a riddle"? In chapter 7, I'll show you how to make up your own riddles, but this one is fun to practice on.

96. I am at the beginning of eternity and the end of time. What am I?

The letter *e*.

97. I move quickly but do not have feet. You can hear me, but I do not have a mouth. What am I?

The wind.

98. The more I dry, the wetter I get. What am I?

A towel.

99. I have branches but no leaves or bark. What am I?

A library.

100. I have rivers but no water, cities but no buildings, roads but no cars. What am I?

A map.

101. I taste better than I smell. What am I?

A tongue.

102. I am so fragile that if you say my name, I break. What am I?

Silence.

103. I shave facial hair every day but am still able to grow an exceptionally long beard. What am I?

A barber.

104. I always reply but have no mouth. What am I?

An echo.

105. The more you take away from me, the larger I get. What am I?

A hole.

106. I am always in front of you, but you cannot see me. What am I?

The future.

107. You can only keep me after giving me to someone else. What am I?

Your word or promise.

108. I have many keys but cannot open a single lock. What am I?

A piano.

109. You can hold me in your right hand but never in your left hand. What am I?

Your left elbow.

110. I have one head, one foot, and four legs. What am I?

A bed.

111. Forward I am heavy, but backward I am not. What am I?

The word "ton."

112. I can go up but can never come down. What am I?

Your age.

113. I am taller when I am sitting than when I am standing. What am I?

A dog.

AROUND THE WORLD

Riddles like these, along with proverbs, are common in Africa, where people use them to share wisdom about things they observe in life and nature.

114. **I can only live in light but disappear if light shines directly on me. What am I?**

A shadow.

115. I am not alive, but I can die. What am I?

A battery.

116. I fly all day but have no wings and never leave my spot. What am I?

A flag.

117. I have a neck but no head, and yet I wear a cap. What am I?

A bottle.

118. I am a seed whose name is three letters long and pronounced the same even when you remove the last two letters. What am I?

A pea.

119. I come alive when I am buried but perish when I'm dug up. What am I?

A plant.

120. I have many ears but cannot hear. What am I?

A cornfield.

121. You can catch me, but you cannot throw me. What am I?

A cold.

122. I am easy to get into but hard to get out of. What am I?

Trouble.

123. I run all around the backyard, but I never move. What am I?

A fence.

124. I am a six-letter word found in many rooms. My first half is an automobile, my last half is a domesticated animal, and my first four letters are a type of fish. What am I?

Carpet.

125. I can build castles and break down mountains. I can blind you yet also help you see. What am I?

Sand.

126. I am always on the table at mealtime, but you do not get to eat me. What am I?

A plate.

127. I have many teeth but cannot bite, chew, or cut. What am I?

A comb.

128. I am black when you buy me, orange when you use me, and gray when you are done with me. What am I?

Charcoal.

129. If you lose me, the people around you will often lose me too. What am I?

Your temper.

130. You see me come down but never go up. What am I?

Rain.

131. I go up and down, but I never move. What am I?

A staircase, or temperature.

132. I am a building with more than 500 stories. What am I?

A library.

133. I am a fruit, a bird, and a person. What am I?

Kiwi.

134. I am not alive, but I need air and can grow. What am I?

A fire.

135. I have a bed, but I never sleep. I have a mouth, but I never eat. What am I?

A river.

136. I have three feet but cannot walk. What am I?

A yardstick.

137. I can fall out of a building and live, but if you put me in fire or water, I will die. What am I?

Paper.

138. I can be cracked, played, and made. What am I?

A joke.

139. I am a number with five letters in my name that appear in alphabetical order. What am I?

Forty.

140. I occur once in a minute, twice in a moment, but never in a thousand years. What am I?

The letter *m*.

141. Why can a man living in Canada not be buried in the United States?

Because he is still living.

142. The more you take of me, the more you leave behind. What am I?

Steps.

143. I have a thumb and four fingers, but I am not a hand. What am I?

A glove.

144. I can fill a room, but I take up no space. What am I?

Light. And laughter!

145. The faster you run, the harder it is to catch me. What am I?

Your breath.

146. I have keys but no doors, space but no rooms, and you can enter but you cannot leave. What am I?

A keyboard.

147. The more there is of me, the less you see. What am I?

Darkness.

148. I have four eyes but cannot see. What am I?

The word Mississippi.

149. What is easy to lift but hard to throw?

A feather.

150. I am noisy when I am changing. After I have changed, I am larger but weigh less. What am I?

Popcorn.

151. You can hold me, but not with your hands. You can bury me, but not underground. What am I?

A grudge or secret.

152. I make two people out of one. What am I?

A mirror.

153. When I am dirty, I am white, but when I am clean, I am green or black. What am I?

A chalkboard.

154. I am an insect. The first half of my name is the name of another insect. What am I?

A beetle.

155. No matter how much rain falls on me, I can never get wetter. What am I?

Water.

156. You throw me out when you need me but bring me in when you do not. What am I?

An anchor.

157. I sometimes run, but I cannot walk. You follow me everywhere. What am I?

Your nose.

158. I am often needed and given, but rarely taken. What am I?

Advice.

159. I come in many shapes, sizes, and colors. I look like I can fit in several different places, but I require one specific place. What am I?

A puzzle piece.

160. I am always in charge and never in debt. I am also the first of my kind. What am I?

The letter a.

161. I grow instantly larger in light and, just as quickly, get smaller in the dark. What am I?

The pupil of an eye.

162. What is at the end of a rainbow that isn't a color?

The letter w.

163. I have been around for thousands of years, but I am never more than one month old. What am I?

The moon.

164. I am the creator of invention and the maker of all adventure. What am I?

Curiosity.

165. I go in circles but travel straight. What am I?

A wheel.

166. I do not have feet, hands, legs, arms, or wings, yet I can crawl under doors or fly high into the sky. What am I?

Smoke.

167. You can take my whole away from me, but I will still have some left. What am I?

The word *wholesome*.

168. I am tall when I am young and short when I'm old. What am I?

A candle.

169. You answer me even though I never ask questions. What am I?

A phone, doorbell, or knock at the door.

170. I always have one eye open. What am I?

A needle.

171. I am light as a feather, but the strongest person in the world cannot hold me for five minutes. What am I?

Your breath.

172. Forward, I am something people do each day. Backward, I am something to fear. What am I?

Live.

173. We can be helpful or hurtful. You can hear us, but you cannot see us or touch us. What are we?

Words.

174. You can serve me, but I cannot be eaten. What am I?

A tennis ball or volleyball.

175. I travel from here to there by appearing, and back from there to here by disappearing. What am I?

The letter *t*.

176. You see me once in October, three times in December, but never in July or August. What am I?

The letter *e*.

177. You can see me but never touch or feel me. No matter how fast you approach me, I am always the same distance away. What am I?

The horizon.

178. I am small, white, and round and served at a table. Either two or four people can enjoy me, but I am never eaten. What am I?

A ping-pong ball.

179. I live on a busy street. When you visit me, it is always to see someone else, so I charge you rent. What am I?

A parking meter.

180. My first half is in the present, my second half in the past. I go up and down but never wander. What am I?

A seesaw.

181. I have two arms and two feet but no fingers or toes. I can carry things easily if my feet do not touch the ground. What am I?

A wheelbarrow.

182. I am always with you, yet you always leave me behind. What am I?

Fingerprints.

183. When I am yours, you can touch me but cannot see me. I can be thrown out but not thrown away. What am I?

A back.

184. I am made of wood but cannot be cut or broken. What am I?

Sawdust.

185. I can be thin but not fat. You consume me but cannot hold me. I am best fresh. What am I?

Air.

186. I build silver bridges and golden crowns. Who am I?

A dentist.

187. Even though I am told what to do at night and reliably do so the next morning, I am often grumbled at and always told to be quiet. What am I?

An alarm clock.

188. I had a bright start but could not take the pressure. I consume everything, but I do not eat anything. What am I?

A black hole.

189. I have a head but no body and leaves but no branches. What am I?

Lettuce.

190. I start sounding like I work for the CIA, then my middle is the middle of middle, and my end is the most-used section of the hospital. What creature am I?

A spider.

> **RIDDLE HISTORY**
>
> Did you recognize this riddle? It's changed up a little, but based on the riddle the Sphinx posed to Harry Potter in *Harry Potter and the Goblet of Fire*.

191. I have many names spelled many ways, but I always have two Xs. What am I?

A woman (with two X chromosomes).

MIX IT UP

This one's a little unfair, because you may not have learned it yet. Try recruiting the help of someone a little older. (Hint: Someone who has taken seventh-grade science.)

PUNS & JOKES

Have you ever heard of a *conundrum*? While some people use the term to describe a difficult problem, it can also be used to describe a riddle that involves a play on words. These types of riddles usually involve *puns*. Puns take advantage of the multiple meanings of a word or draw connections between words that sound similar. Some answers include similar-sounding words, like *please* or *peas* instead of *peace*.

Conundrums are typically meant to be funny, but they're also really tricky. You'll need to put on your thinking cap to make sense of the punny business in this chapter!

192. What bird is with you at breakfast, lunch, and dinner?

A swallow.

193. What did the angry cake say to the fork?

You want a piece of me?

194. What type of bone will a dog never eat?

A trombone.

195. What kind of lion never roars?

A dandelion.

196. What do you call an alligator in a vest?

An investigator.

197. What is fast, crunchy, and can travel far?

A rocket chip.

198. What did the quartz say to the geologist?

Don't take me for granite.

199. Why did the eighth grader bring a ladder to class?

Because she wanted to be in high school.

200. Why did the students eat their homework?

Because the teacher said it was a piece of cake.

201. What did the left eye say to the right eye?

Between you and me, something smells.

202. What do you call a cow that has had a baby?

De-calf-einated.

203. Why shouldn't you start a conversation with pi?

Because it goes on and on forever.

204. How did the rabbit travel?

By hare plane.

205. Why was the jalapeño wearing a sweater?

Because it was a little chile (chilly).

206. What do you call a bear with no teeth?

A gummy bear.

207. What was wrong with the tree's car?

It wooden go.

208. Where does a peacock go when he loses his tail?

A re-tail store.

209. What do you call a sleeping stegosaurus?

A dino-snore.

210. Why did the chef wear a helmet whenever he was cooking?

Because he was on a crash diet.

211. What do clouds wear under their raincoats?

Thunderwear.

212. What do cows do for fun?

Go to the moo-vies.

213. What do you call a sad strawberry?

A blue berry.

214. Why couldn't the moon finish his meal?

He was full.

215. What else can you call a grandfather clock?

An old timer.

216. Where do salmon keep their money?

In a riverbank.

217. What do you get when you combine a vampire with a snowman?

Frost bite.

218. Where do monkeys work out?

At the jungle gym.

219. What day do Easter eggs hate?

Fry-day.

220. Why did the fraction ⅕ need a massage?

Because it was two-tenths.

221. What are a squirrel's favorite flowers?

Forget-me-nuts.

222. What is an astronaut's favorite meal?

Launch.

223. What is a sheep's favorite sport?

Baa-dminton.

224. Who won the skeleton beauty pageant?

No body.

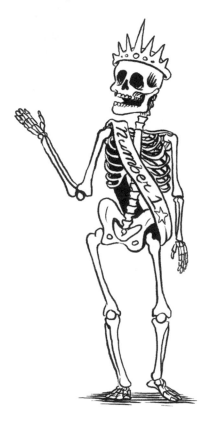

225. Why did the author install a knocker on her door?

Because she wanted to win the no-bell prize.

226. When is a door not a door?

When it's ajar.

227. What do you call two bananas?

Slippers.

228. What did the plate say to the spoon?

Dinner is on me.

229. Why did the child cross the playground?

To get to the other slide.

230. What was the wizard's favorite subject in school?

Spelling.

231. How much do pirates pay to get their ears pierced?

A buck an ear.

232. What did the parent volcano say to the baby volcano?

I lava you.

233. How do you make jellyfish laugh?

With ten tickles.

> **SILLY STATS**
>
> Jellyfish have been around for millions of years. (They were around before dinosaurs!) Some types have hundreds of tentacles.

234. How does a scientist freshen his breath?

With experi-mints.

235. How can you tell when a vampire has caught a cold?

He starts coffin.

236. Why are chemists great problem solvers?

Because they have all the solutions.

237. How does a cucumber become a pickle?

It goes through a jarring experience.

238. Why couldn't the pony sing its favorite song?

Because it was a little horse.

239. Why does the sun refuse to go to school?

Because it already has a million degrees.

240. Why did the banana go to the doctor?

Because it wasn't peeling well.

241. What do you call a funny mountain?

Hill-arious.

242. What do you call a rubber spaghetti noodle?

An impasta.

243. How do you throw a party in outer space?

You planet.

244. What do you get when you combine a centipede with a parrot?

A walkie talkie.

245. What did zero say to eight?

Nice belt.

246. What is a frog's favorite food?

French flies.

247. Why did the crouton blush?

It saw the salad dressing.

248. Why was the painting arrested?

Because it was framed.

249. Why do porcupines always win at basketball and football but never golf?

Because they always have the most points.

250. Why was the broom late?

It over-swept.

251. Why were clocks banned from the library?

Because they tock too much.

252. **Where do sheep go on vacation?**

The Baa-hamas.

253. What did the history book say to the math book?

You've got problems!

254. Why did the museum curator decide to become an archeologist?

Because her career was in ruins.

255. Have you heard the one about the girl who is afraid of negative numbers?

She'll stop at nothing to avoid them.

256. Name two ways to stop a bull from charging.

1) Take away its credit card.

2) Unplug its power cord.

257. Which days are the strongest?

Saturday and Sunday because the rest are week days.

258. Which letter of the alphabet holds the most water?

The *C*.

259. Why was Cinderella thrown off the basketball team?

Because she ran away from the ball.

260. What did one charged atom say to the other?

I've got my ion you.

261. What kind of advice can you get from your hand?

Finger tips.

262. What is a math teacher's favorite dessert?

Pi.

263. What kind of button cannot be unbuttoned?

A belly button.

264. What did the cheese say when it looked in the mirror?

Looking gouda.

265. Why did the duck stop in the middle of the road?

Because it tripped on a quack.

266. How did courageous Egyptians record their adventures?

Hero-glyphics.

267. What are a pirate's least favorite vegetable?

Leeks.

268. What is the best time to go to the dentist?

Tooth-hurty.

269. Why can't you win an argument against a 90-degree angle?

Because it's always right.

270. What is a snake's favorite subject?

Hiss-tory.

271. Why was the baby strawberry crying?

Because her parents were in a jam.

272. Why is it impossible to make a reservation at the library?

Because they're always booked.

273. What do you call a cow that plays the harp?

A moo-sician.

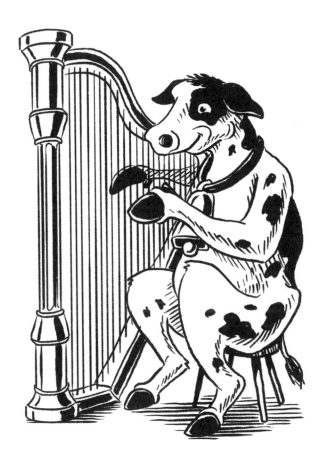

274. What happened when oxygen went on a date with potassium?

It went OK.

275. What did the cartoonist say to his rival?

I challenge you to a doodle.

276. What kind of flower grows on your face?

Tulips.

277. Why did the thief rob the bakery?

Because there's a lot of dough.

278. Why do trees hate riddles?

Because they don't like to be stumped.

279. What do you call a dinosaur with a large vocabulary?

A thesaurus.

280. What do you call witches who share a house?

Broom-mates.

281. How do you catch a school of fish?

With a bookworm.

282. What is the strongest sea creature?

A mussel.

SILLY STATS

Mussel is the punny answer, but the real answer is the Australian Saltwater Crocodile. They can clamp their jaws shut with a force of 3,700 pounds per square inch, more than twice the strength of a hippo!

283. What did the beach say when the tide came in?

Long time, no sea.

284. What do you call a fairy that needs a bath?

Stinker bell.

285. Why can't a bicycle stand on its own?

Because it's two tired.

286. What did the townspeople call the person who only spoke in figurative language?

The Village Idiom.

287. A man is locked in a room with no windows or doors. The only items in the room are a mirror and a table. How is he able to escape? (Remember, this chapter is about puns!)

He looks in the mirror to see what he saw. He takes the saw and cuts the table in half. Next, he puts the two halves together to form a whole. Then, he simply crawls out of the room through the hole.

4

BRAIN TEASERS

(Answers begin on page 113.)

Brain teasers are puzzles that exercise your lateral thinking skills. This means you need to use creativity *and* examine the problem from multiple angles to find the answer. Technically, all the riddles in this book are brain teasers. But now that we've warmed up your creative thinking skills, we are going to tackle more challenging ones. Some might take extra time, but they're not impossible. Keep an eye out for some new tricks. At times you'll be using the information presented at face value, but other times you will need to look at the words to find patterns.

The brain teasers in this chapter will include more details. This time, you'll find the answers at the back of the book (see page 113), to make it more challenging. You'll have to take all of the information into consideration and reason through it to a solution. These riddles are especially fun to work on in groups. Work together to solve them, or team up and see which team can solve the riddles fastest!

288. What word can come before the following: bag, box, and paper?

289. Mrs. Johnson baked a dozen cookies. Her 12 children came to the kitchen. Each took a cookie and left. There are 11 cookies remaining. How is this possible?

290. How is it that a typical horse can run 30 kilometers with two of its legs but 31 kilometers with the other two?

291. The 25th Amendment to the US Constitution outlines how presidential succession should be handled. If both the vice president and the Speaker of the House pass away, who becomes president?

292. Four people sat down to play together one night. They played for hours. They each had similar scores, and at the end of the evening, they each made a profit. How is it possible for all four to have made money?

293. Mr. Martinez walks into the kitchen to make breakfast. The refrigerator contains bacon, eggs, milk, and jelly. What does he open first?

294. A man works on the 42nd floor. Any time he rides the elevator alone, he goes up to the 32nd floor of his building, then walks the remaining 10 stories. When other people are in the elevator, he rides all the way up to the 42nd floor. At the end of the workday, he gets on the elevator on the 42nd floor and rides it all the way down to the lobby. He isn't taking the stairs to get exercise. Why does he get off on the 32nd floor instead of riding the elevator all the way to the 42nd floor?

295. In the town of Fibster, the townspeople always lie. In the town of Verity, the townspeople always tell the truth. It's also a law that groups of two or more must always contain at least one person from each town. At the Fibster park, you meet a boy and a girl. The boy says, "I'm Benjamin and this is my friend Imani. One of us lives in Verity." Is Benjamin telling the truth or is he fibbing?

296. How is it possible to stay underwater longer than an Olympic swimmer who can hold his breath for three minutes, without any special breathing apparatus? (Hint: It has nothing to do with technique.)

297. Which of the following numbers comes next in this series: 6, 4, 3, 11, 15, ... ?

Is it 7, 12, 17, or 20?

298. If you have seven sugar cubes that look exactly the same but have been told that one of them weighs just a little more than the others, how can you find the heavier cube by using a balance scale no more than two times?

299. A seven-letter word can be broken into two other words, and, keeping letters in the same order, be used in the following sentence: A _____ surgeon had _____ and as a result, was _____ to operate. What is the word?

300. Can you find what is unusual about this paragraph? It may look normal to you, but it is truly abnormal. As soon as you grasp it, you'll know a surprising fact. What is odd about this paragraph? Good luck! I know you can do it!

AROUND THE WORLD

E isn't just the most commonly used letter in English, it's also the most common in Dutch, Finnish, French, German, Hungarian, Italian, Norwegian, Spanish, and Swedish.

---

301. In a town with only two barbers, which barber should you go to for the best haircut—the one with a fantastic haircut or the one with a poor haircut?

302. A palindrome is a word or phrase that is spelled the same forward and backward. Can you think of a seven-letter palindrome that describes what you should do when a specific type of tool gets dirty?

303. Two clever siblings were trying to decide who would get the last cookie. The brother suggested that he could write the words "Yes" and "No" on two different pieces of paper. If his sister randomly chose the paper that said "Yes," she could have the last cookie. The sister worried that the brother might write "No" on both pieces of paper, making it impossible for her to select one that said "Yes." How could she succeed in getting the last cookie if her brother was already holding the pieces of paper in each hand?

304. Three kids are debating how much candy their parents have hidden. Ellie says, "Mom and Dad have at least 20 candy bars stashed away." Johnathan says, "They definitely have fewer than 20 candy bars hidden." And Katie says, "I know they are hiding at least one candy bar from us." Only one of their statements is true. Who is correct and how many candy bars do their parents have?

305. How is it possible for a car facing east to travel five miles in a straight line and end up west of where it started?

306. At the local bakery, a pie costs $6, cake costs $8, and bread costs $10. How much does a cookie cost?

307. What letter can replace the last letter of the following words: rub, bard, crows, cat?

308. According to the US Constitution, in order to become president, a candidate must be at least 35 years old, be a US citizen, have lived in the United States for at least 14 years, and be born in the United States. There is one last requirement a candidate must meet. What is it?

309. In the town of Fibster, the townspeople always lie. In the town of Verity, the townspeople always tell the truth. You meet three people at the border between the two towns and ask "Which town are you each from?" The first person whispers his response so you can't hear. The second person says, "He said he is from Verity. So am I." The third person says, "They are both from Fibster, but I'm from Verity." Which town is each of the three people from?

310. Oscar, an aspiring magician, decided on a very daring feat for his first magic trick. For his first performance, he walked across a lake without any special equipment. He succeeded in his task without getting wet, but the audience was not impressed. Why not?

311. Mason's grandfather was showing him his collection of historical memorabilia. In part of his collection, he has a newspaper dated November 11, 1918 with the headline "World War I Is Over." He also has some ancient scrolls dated 132 BCE. Mason told him that, unfortunately, those two items were worthless. Why?

312. When Mrs. Yang walked into the kitchen, she found a broken glass shattered on the floor. She immediately went to the family room to find out why whoever dropped the glass hadn't cleaned it up. As she entered the room she asked, "Who made the mess in the kitchen and didn't clean it up?" Her son Michael replied, "I haven't been in the kitchen all day." Her daughter Ava said, "It must have been Claire since she's drinking a glass of water right now!" To which Claire responded, "I didn't make the mess! The kitchen looked fine when I was in there." Who is the guilty party?

313. If you change one letter, what do the following words have in common: worth, mouth, last, best?

314. Imagine six glasses lined up in a single row. The first three are filled with water and the last three are empty. By moving only one glass, how can you arrange the glasses so that the empty and full glasses alternate? (Hint: Get creative on how and what you move.)

315. Tia tells you that she is going to the park with her father's sister's only sister-in-law's son. Who is she going to the park with?

316. There is a glass bottle sealed with a cork. Inside the bottle is a precious gemstone worth thousands of dollars. You can keep the gem if you can remove it from the bottle without breaking the glass or taking the cork out of the bottle. How do you get the gemstone out?

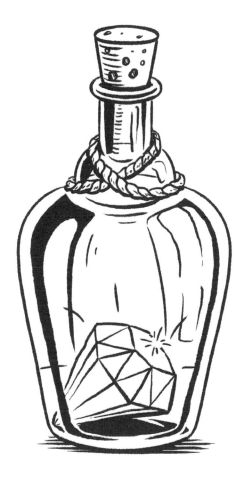

317. What four letter word can be used before the words house and sandwich and after the words book and golf?

318. The 22nd president of the United States had the same parents as the 24th president of the United States, but the 22nd and 24th president were not brothers. How is this possible? (Hint: This is fact!)

319. Yesterday, Jung walked all around town. Each time he encountered someone he would ask them a question. The question he asked was always the same. Occasionally, he would run into someone he had already encountered earlier in the day and would ask them the question again. He never received the same answer twice. What was his question?

320. What do the following words have in common: civic, madam, rotator, tenet?

321. One, Two, Three, Four, and Five are in class together. The math teacher sends Three to the principal's office for bad behavior. What was Three doing?

322. Ms. Reed has a terrible memory. She was worried she wouldn't be able to remember her computer password, which is a random assortment of letters and numbers, so she created a password hint that was foolproof. The hint is: You force heaven to be empty. What is her password?

323. If Marisa travels by car, Valerie walks, and Ivan takes the train, who rides a bicycle, Arjun or Lucas? (Hint: Look at letter patterns.)

324. What do the following words have in common: banana, dresser, grammar, potato, uneven?

325. A rich man wants to leave his inheritance to the smartest of his three children. To determine which child was wisest, he challenged them to see which son could fill the empty guest room by spending the least amount of money filling it. The first son spent $300 on a bounce house that filled the room. The second son spent $100 on 1,000 balloons to fill the room. The third son won by spending just $10. What did he buy to fill the room?

326. A group of players from the same baseball team head to the park to play a game. The final score is 7 to 7. No player touched any bases, nor did they hit any runs. How is this possible?

327. In the town of Fibster, the townspeople always lie. In the town of Verity, the townspeople always tell the truth. While getting ice cream at a truck halfway between the two cities, you want to know if the person behind you is from Fibster or Verity. To find out, you ask her to ask the person behind her in line which town he is from. You can't hear the person behind her answer, but she tells you he said he is from Verity. Is the person behind you from Fibster or Verity?

328. Which of the following sentences doesn't belong? (Hint: It's not the meaning of the sentences.)

a) Dev outran Greg.
b) Clara ate tuna.
c) Fred is silly.
d) Brianna is really driven.

329. In the town of Fibster, the townspeople always lie. In the town of Verity, the townspeople always tell the truth. On a trip to visit Verity, you come to a fork in the road, and the sign post is missing to direct you the right way. Luckily, a townsperson is there. Since you don't know which town the person is from, what can you ask him in order to know which way to go?

330. What word do the following words have in common: fall, front, melon, ski, tower?

331. What word is missing from the following sequence?

Fin, inch, chest, stew, _____ , web

332. Can you find the name of a country hidden in the following sentences?

I love to sit outside to enjoy the sun and the wind. I am an outdoor person for sure!

333. Zara was traveling to the local farmers' market along Main Street. On the way there, she met a family with eight children. Each child held two bags. Each bag held three fish. How many people were traveling to the farmers' market?

RIDDLE HISTORY

This riddle was inspired by the "As I was going to St. Ives" riddle, which was found in a book written in 1730. The original riddle is: "As I was going to St. Ives, I met a man with seven wives. Each wife had seven sacks, each sack had seven cats, each cat had seven kits: kits, cats, sacks, and wives, how many were going to St. Ives?" (The answer there is one as well!)

---

334. Hiroshi is having a birthday party and his mother has already sliced the cake into eight slices. Just before the cake is served, the neighbors swing by and now the party has doubled in size. Hiroshi's mother manages to slice the cake into 16 pieces by making only *one* more cut. How does she manage this?

335. There are three switches by the front door that control three different light bulbs in the basement. How can you figure out which light switch controls each light bulb if you can only make one trip to the basement?

5

FUN WITH MATH

(Answers begin on page 119.)

Math is a great way to practice problem solving and critical thinking. It takes logic, looking for patterns, and methodically working through each step. When armed with strong math skills, we can create order from chaos. It's how construction workers turn a pile of wood into a home, or how a chef turns a bag of groceries into a gourmet meal.

The riddles in this chapter are going to help you flex your math muscles. There are no trick questions, and once again you'll find the answers at the back of the book (see page 119). You should be able to solve each riddle by using basic math. The only challenge is figuring out which of your math skills to use for each problem. Grab a pencil and paper. They'll help you work out some of the more challenging riddles ahead. Some hints are offered, but try to use them only if you're stumped.

336. 20 + 20 + 20 = 60.

How can you get to the sum of 60 with three identical digits that *aren't* 20?

337. What is the three-digit number where the following are true: the first digit is one more than the last, the second is greater than the first and last, and the sum of all three digits is 16? Start by experimenting with different numbers, placing them where they might fit the description.

338. How many times does the digit 8 occur between 0 and 100? (Hint: This is trickier than you think!)

339. All the digits from 1 to 9 are used in the equation below. Can you fill in the blanks? (Hint: Start with information you know must be true. What combinations are possible to get the given answer so far? Once you figure out the first number, go from there.)

__ 6 __ + 3 __ 7 = __ 1 __

340. What number is missing in the following sequence? (Hint: Think creatively, not necessarily mathematically.)

16, 06, 68, 88, ___, 98

341. If four painters can paint four rooms in two days, how long will it take one painter to paint six rooms?

342. If you walk to your friend's house at five miles per hour, discover he's not home, and return home walking at three miles per hour, how far away does your friend live if the total trip took you 48 minutes? (Hint: Your pace on the way to your friend's house was 12 minutes per mile, and on the way back it was 20 minutes per mile.)

343. Sebastian brought some snacks to share with Zain and Randall. The snacks were divided equally between all three friends. Each of the friends ate half of their snacks. Then, Zain ate one-fourth of his remaining snacks. Sebastian ate three-fourths of his remaining snacks, leaving him with just two. Randall ate one-eighth of his remaining snacks. How many snacks did they start with? (Hint: Look at the second sentence. The number must be equally divided by three, and large enough for there to be leftovers.)

344. Sofia has two more sisters than she has brothers. Her brother Val has three times as many sisters as brothers. There are fewer than 10 children in the family. How many are girls and how many are boys? (Hint: You can experiment by starting at nine [fewer than 10 children] and going backward, or starting at one brother and multiplying by two until you get to an even number under 10.)

345. Miguel is 12 years old. Mia is half Miguel's age. How old will Mia be when Miguel is 100?

346. Three hot dogs and four bottles of water cost $10. Two hot dogs and two bottles of water cost $6. What is the price of each hot dog and each bottle of water? Try experimenting with different prices.

347. Marion is four times the age that Jamie was three years ago. In two more years, Marion will be double Jamie's current age. Added together, their ages today equal 13. How old is each of them? (Hint: Start with what you know, which is their total current age, and work from there. What age splits are possible today? What are their current minimum ages?)

348. In the problems below, each letter stands for a different digit. If T = 8, can you figure out the value of the rest of the letters?

CAT + DOG = PET

PAN + DOG = TEN

> **MIX IT UP**
>
> See if you can make another equation with real words using the same letter assignments from this riddle. You don't have to stick with three-letter words or addition.

349. Adrien and Amari decide to bet on coin tosses. Each time the coin lands on heads, Amari must pay Adrien $1. If the coin lands on tails, Adrien must pay Amari $1. When they are done, Adrien has won three times, but Amari ends with $5. How many times did they flip the coin?

350. By looking at the pattern below, can you figure out which number comes next?

2, 3, 5, 8, 12, ?

> **MIX IT UP**
>
> Make a contest out of solving sequences by racing a friend or family member to see who can find the answer fastest!

351. Place +, -, ×, and ÷ in between the numbers below to make an equation that is correct. Solve the equation left to right (ignore typical mathematical order of operations). All four symbols must be used once.

2 __ 9 __ 3 __ 1 __ 4 = 8

> **MIX IT UP**
>
> We ignore the order of operations for this problem to make it easier to solve. This wouldn't be correct on a math test! Remember to always multiply and divide before you add and subtract.

352. If Wyatt buys a baseball card for $5 and sells it to Rory for $7, but later buys it back for $10, only to sell it again for $12, how much profit does he make, if any?

353. A music teacher needs to order recorders for his students. Knowing he would need over 100, when the math teacher asked how many he was ordering, the music teacher decided to have some fun with his reply. He said:

- If I order in twos, I'll be short one recorder.

- If I order in groups of three, I'll be short two recorders.

- If I order in groups of four, I'll be short three recorders.

- If I order in groups of five, I'll be short four recorders.

- If I order in groups of six, I'll be short five recorders.

- I must order in groups of seven to obtain just the right amount.

How many recorders will he order?

354. Imagine you have a box in front of you filled with $1, $5, $10, and $20 bills. You are allowed to take one bill at a time from the box until you have taken four bills of the same value (e.g., four $10 bills). What is the most money you can possibly draw before accomplishing this?

355. What is the four-digit number where the following are true: the first digit is double the second, the third is half of the fourth, the second is less than the third, and the sum of the digits is 15?

356. If a tree doubles in height every year until it reaches its maximum height at 10 years, how many years does it take for the tree to reach half of its maximum height? (Hint: It's not five years.)

SILLY STATS

The Empress tree is the fastest growing hardwood tree in the world. It grows up to 20 feet its first year and can reach a height of up to 50 feet!

---

357. Mrs. Wilson washed a bunch of cherries and set them in a large bowl for her three children to snack on. When Alex noticed them on the counter, he ate one-third to leave equal portions for his brother and sister. Later, Alyssa discovered the cherries and, not realizing Alex had already eaten some, only ate one-third to leave enough for her brothers. When Tyler saw the cherries, he also only ate one-third to be sure to save some for his siblings. If there were eight cherries left after Tyler had eaten his share, how many cherries were in the bowl at the beginning? (Hint: Remember eight is one-third of what Tyler started with before he ate his share.)

358. What two digits create a one-digit answer if they are multiplied together but a two-digit answer if they are added together?

359. Notice 2 + 2 = 4 and 2 × 2 = 4. Find three whole numbers, each a different digit, that equal the same number whether they're added together or multiplied.

360. When Mr. Malik slammed on his brakes to avoid hitting a mother goose crossing the road with her six goslings, it caused a 10-car bumper-to-bumper pile-up accident behind him. How many bumpers were damaged in the accident?

361. What is ½ of ⅔ of ¾ of ⅘ of ⅚ of ⁶/₇ of ⅞ of ⁸/₉ of ⁹/₁₀ of 1000? (Hint: Start at the end.)

362. Mateo, Samia, and Nikki are hungry and craving hamburgers for lunch. Unfortunately, their grill can only fit two hamburger patties at one time. Since each side takes five minutes to cook, it will be 20 minutes before all three hamburgers are done. Mateo realizes there's a way to completely cook all three burgers in just 15 minutes. Can you figure out how?

363. Ms. Brown has a grandfather clock that chimes every hour on the hour and at every half hour. On the half hour, it always chimes once. At each hour, it chimes according to the time (i.e., one chime at one o'clock, two chimes at two o'clock, three chimes at three o'clock, etc.). If Ms. Brown arrives home and hears a chime as she enters, another chime 30 minutes later, and one chime after another 30 minutes, what time did Ms. Brown arrive home?

RIDDLE HISTORY

Grandfather clocks are named after a song written in 1875 by an American songwriter. He wrote the song "My Grandfather's Clock" about a clock at an inn he'd visited that stopped working at the exact time the inn's owner passed away.

364. When you add Harper's age to her mother's, the sum is 55. Harper's age is the reverse of her mother's. How old is Harper and how hold is her mother? (Note: Harper is a teenager.)

365. Carter loves animals. All his pets are dogs except two. Oddly, all his pets are cats except two. Stranger yet, all his pets are birds except two. How many pets does Carter have?

366. There are 20 socks in a laundry basket. Ten of the socks are white and 10 of the socks are gray. If you were blindfolded, what is the fewest number of socks you could pick from the basket to be certain you were holding a matching pair?

367. If we know a pencil costs $1 more than an eraser, and that together they cost $1.20, can you figure out how much an eraser costs purchased separately? (Hint: It's not 20 cents!)

368. In the puzzle below, each letter stands for a different digit. If F = 9, can you figure out which numbers each of the other letters represents?

FUN – ONE = HON

BUT – NO = BOW

369. If it takes one child 30 seconds to sharpen a pencil, how long does it take three children to sharpen 12 pencils, assuming each child has their own pencil sharpener?

370. Kai and Carmen go to the beach to collect shark teeth. They agree to split the shark teeth evenly at the end of the day so each has the same number. When they are done, they realize that if Kai gives Carmen one tooth, Carmen will have twice as many as Kai. However, if Carmen gives Kai one tooth, they'll have an equal number. How many shark teeth did each person collect?

371. Kabir is trying to climb a hill that is 150 feet tall. Unfortunately, the hill is very muddy, so for every three feet Kabir travels forward, he slides back one foot. How many feet total will Kabir have walked by the time he reaches the top of the hill?

372. Mrs. Palmer likes to boil her tea for exactly seven minutes. Being rather old-fashioned, she doesn't have a regular kitchen timer, but instead uses hourglass timers. She has a 3-minute timer, a 5-minute timer, and a 10-minute timer. How can she use her available timers to make sure she boils her tea for exactly seven minutes?

373. What number comes next in the series?

1, 3, 6, 10, 15, 21, ?

374. Aaron has 100 pennies. He distributes the coins into four different bags. Each bag has two more pennies than the bag filled before it. How many pennies are in each bag?

375. In front of you are three bags, each containing two marbles. You know that one bag contains two white marbles, one bag contains two black marbles, and that the third bag contains one white marble and one black marble, but you don't know which bag contains which marbles. If you pick a bag at random and remove a white marble, is it more likely or less likely that the other marble in the bag is white?

376. A fox is 10 yards away from a rabbit when it begins chasing it. The rabbit is 40 yards away from its hole. The fox can run 5 yards per second, but the rabbit can only run 4 yards per second. Will the rabbit make it to its hole before the fox catches it?

> **MIX IT UP**
>
> Another way to solve this problem would be to make a graph that shows the rabbit's and fox's starting locations and mark their progress after each second.

377. The digits 1, 2, and 3 have been randomly assigned to the letters A, B, and C. Using the clues below, can you determine which letters symbolize which digits?

BCBA is smaller than ABAB, which is smaller than CABC. The sum of the digits in the largest number is 9.

378. Aubrey is building a house of cards using eight decks of cards (a total of 416 cards). On the first day, she places 162 cards. To avoid making it collapse, each day she places only two-thirds of the number of cards as the day before. How many days will it take to complete her house of cards?

379. What is the four-digit number where the following are true: the second digit is double the third, the first is greater than the last, the last is the smallest, and the sum of the digits is 15?

380. Place +, -, ×, and ÷ in between the numbers below to make an equation that is correct. Solve the equation left to right (ignore the typical mathematical order of operations). All four symbols must be used once.

4 __ 3 __ 6 __ 8 __ 1 = 9

381. Omar and Kam go to buy school supplies and agree to share the items and the expense. Omar buys a package of pencil grips for $1. Kam buys some stickers for $2 and a pack of markers for $4. How much does Omar owe Kam?

382. Can you figure out the pattern in the following sequence sets to determine the missing number?

| 4, 3, 2 | 10, 6, 8 | 15, 7, 16 |
| 7, 5, 4 | 8, 1, 14 | 12, 3, ? |

BRAIN BENDER

383. Theo's parents decide to give him an allowance. It will start out at $5 per month but will increase by $1 every month. Emery's parents also decide to start paying a similar allowance but decide to pay her twice a month. So, Emery's allowance starts at $2.50 and will increase by 25 cents every time she gets paid. Who will make more money in the first three months? Who will make more money at the end of one year?

LOGIC PUZZLES

(Answers begin on page 126.)

I've saved my very favorite type of riddles for last: logic puzzles! To solve the riddles in this chapter, you're going to use deductive reasoning to eliminate options until you reach the correct solution. You will have to pay close attention to details in order to solve these puzzles. And again, you'll find the answers at the back of the book (page 126).

Like the math challenges in the preceding chapter, these puzzles aren't meant to trick you. They're intended to exercise your deductive reasoning. You should give yourself a pat on the back for each logic puzzle you complete. The skills required to solve them are hard to master, but they will benefit you for the rest of your life!

384. Can you think of a four-letter word that describes a way you communicate and that, when you change the third letter, becomes something you must do?

385. Five friends each have a different favorite class at school. Can you use the clues below to figure out which class is each friend's favorite?

- Neither Samir nor Kendall like science, and Samir also dislikes reading.
- Harley's favorite subject is music.
- Eden's favorite subject is either math or science.
- Drew enjoys social studies the most.

386. There is one letter that, if added to each of the following four-letter words, will form three new five-letter words. What is the letter?

     CHAT   BLOW   REST

387. Complete the following analogy: Scarf is to neck as ring is to _____.

Is the correct answer hand, finger, glove, or phone?

388. Paris, Raven, and Corey are friends. One friend plays soccer, another plays baseball, and one plays basketball. Use the clues below to figure out who plays which sport.

* The baseball player doesn't have any siblings and doesn't own a bicycle.

* Paris rides her bicycle to soccer practice with Corey's brother.

RIDDLE HISTORY

This riddle is the most common type of logic puzzle. They often include grids where you can eliminate options based on the clues to narrow in on the solution. Try using grids for the puzzles in this book!

---

389. Mr. Williams lives about an hour from the closest town, so he only goes into town once a week. When he goes to town, he goes to the bank to withdraw cash for shopping, the market to pick up vegetables, the butcher to get meat, and the bakery for fresh bread. The bank is open Monday through Friday. The market is closed on Thursday or Friday. The butcher is open on Tuesday, Thursday, and Saturday. And the bakery is open every day except Wednesday. What day does Mr. Williams go to town to run his errands?

390. Five children decided to race across the park. Lulu finished before Dani, but after Mila. Owen got to the finish line before Elijah, but after Dani. What order did the children finish in?

391. There are four houses of four different colors (red, blue, yellow, and green). In each house lives a person from a different country (England, Japan, Kenya, and Mexico). Each homeowner has a different pet (dog, cat, bird, and fish). Using the following clues, can you tell who owns the fish?

- The person from England lives in the red house.

- The person from Mexico has a cat.

- The owner of the green house has a dog.

- Neither the Japanese person nor the Kenyan owns a bird.

- The owner of the blue house is not from Mexico or Japan.

RIDDLE HISTORY

Rumor has it that a riddle very similar to this was created by Albert Einstein (the original riddle has five houses, five people, five pets, and a couple of other unique characteristics). Other people say the original riddle was written by Lewis Carroll, the author of *Alice's Adventures in Wonderland*.

392. A farmer is traveling with his dog, a rabbit, and some lettuce he is delivering to a friend. He reaches a river that he will have to cross, but the boat on the riverbank will only fit him and one other item. He cannot leave the dog alone with the rabbit, nor can he leave the rabbit alone with the lettuce. How can he transport all three across the river safely in the boat? (Hint: He makes more than one trip.)

393. In Min-seo's class, 12 students had red in their shirts, 10 students had blue in their shirts, and 6 students had yellow in their shirts. Of those students, 8 had both red and blue in their shirts, 3 had red and yellow, and 1 had red, blue, and yellow in their shirt. How many students were wearing solid colored shirts? How many of the solid colored shirts were red? How many were blue? How many were yellow?

394. Jules has a bowl of chocolate-covered candies. The following statements about it are true:

- All the candies with peanuts inside are red.

- Jules likes all the candies in the bowl.

- Jules does not like red candies.

Are there any candies with peanuts in the bowl?

395. Find words that rhyme with each of the words below. The first word is a category. The three words after that are words that fit within that category.

- The name of the category rhymes with SLUMBER.

- The words in the category rhyme with GATE, SIGN, and HEN.

What are the words?

396. Mr. and Mrs. Smith have three daughters and one son. Each of their children has a different favorite color: red, blue, green, or yellow. Likewise, each child has a unique favorite fruit: bananas, cherries, kiwi, or oranges. Can you figure out which child has which preferences based on the facts below?

- Their daughter Joyce likes blue and doesn't like bananas or kiwi.

- Another daughter, Ruby, likes a color that is made by combining her brother's favorite color with one of her sister's favorite colors.

- Camilla's favorite fruit's color is also her favorite color, unlike Isaac's favorite fruit and color.

397. Can you think of a five-letter word that represents a mode of transportation, which, when you change the last letter, becomes something that grows in dirt?

398. Complete the following analogy: Acorn is to forest as seed is to _____.

Is the correct answer fruit, tree, orchard, or plant?

399. There is one letter that, if added to each of the following four-letter words, will form three new five-letter words. What is the letter? (Hint: The letter doesn't have to go in the same place.)

RUBY   THIN   SURE

400. The word DAYBREAK is interesting because not only can it be broken into two words by separating DAY from BREAK, but you can also form two new words by separating its odd and even letters. If you take each of its odd letters (DYRA), you can rearrange them into a new word. Likewise, if you take all its even letters, you can rearrange them to make a different word. What are the two words?

401. Four explorers decide to explore a cave. Just as they reach a bridge that leads to the cave, their flashlight batteries die. Thankfully, one of the explorers has a backup flashlight, though it will only work for 15 minutes. Only two people can be on the bridge at one time. Each of the explorers walks at a different pace. Chloe can cross the bridge in just one minute, but it takes Amit two minutes to cross. Maliah needs five minutes to cross and Oliver needs a full eight minutes to get across the bridge. If two people walk across together, they will travel at the slower person's speed. How can they all get across the bridge in 15 minutes before the flashlight goes out? (Yes, it's possible! Hint: The fastest explorers will cross first and last.)

402. Complete the following analogy: Hungry is to food as dry is to _____.

Is the correct answer wet, desert, hot, or moisture?

403. When cleaning up his classroom, Mr. Jackson accidentally sorted his pencils and erasers into bins with the wrong labels. One bin is labeled "PENCILS," another bin is labeled "ERASERS," and the third bin is labeled "PENCILS & ERASERS." None of the bins have been sorted correctly, so each of the three bins bears the wrong label. Without looking in the bins, how could you correct the labels by removing only one item from one bin?

404. A family of four (two parents and two children) is on a backpacking trip, and they reach a river. A kind fisherman offers to let the family use his small boat to make the crossing. Unfortunately, the boat is only large enough to hold one adult or two children. How can the family use the boat to make the crossing and return the boat to the fisherman? (Hint: There are more than 10 trips across the water!)

AROUND THE WORLD

This riddle is similar to one that is supposedly an IQ test given to job applicants for certain jobs in Japan. In that version there is also a thief and a policeman, adding even more complexity to the puzzle!

---

405. By changing one letter in each of the words below, you can turn the words into two new words that are antonyms of each other. What are the two words you can create?

KEEP   SWALLOW

406. Can you think of a four-letter word that describes a mild temperature, which, when you change the first letter, becomes a place people like to visit in the summer?

407. Can you change the word WARM to COLD in four steps by only changing one letter in the word at a time so that each change creates a real word? (There will be a total of three words in between.) It's called a word ladder. (Hint: The first letter change is a consonant.)

408. The word INTEREST is interesting because if you take each of its odd letters, you can rearrange them into a new word. Likewise, if you take all its even letters, you can rearrange them to make a different word. What are the two words?

409. Complete the following analogy: Pencil is to write as broom is to _____.

Is the correct answer mop, dustpan, sweep, or dirt?

410. Dominique, Aidan, Yuki, and Zara all have birthdays this month. They will be turning 5, 8, 10, and 12, but not in that order. For their gifts, one of them is getting a puppy, one is getting a bike, one is getting a video game, and one is getting clothes. Can you figure out how old each person is turning and what they are getting for their birthday using the clues below?

- The 10-year-old is getting the bike.
- Dominique, who is the youngest, is not getting a puppy.
- The clothes are going to the oldest person, who is not Aidan.
- Yuki, who is not the oldest, is getting a puppy.

411. Find words that rhyme with each of the words below. The first word is a category. The three words after that are words that fit within that category.

- The name of the category rhymes with PINK.
- The words in the category rhyme with SILK, DAUGH-TER, and TRUCE.

What are the words?

412. The word DISLOYAL is interesting because you can take each of its odd letters and rearrange them into a new word. Likewise, you can take all its even letters and rearrange them to make a different word. What are the two words?

413. Violet, Magenta, and Rose showed up at a party in new dresses. Violet said, "Isn't it funny that we are wearing dresses that match our names, but none of us is wearing a dress that matches our own name?" The girl in the rose-colored dress looked around and said, "That is funny!" What color was each girl wearing?

414. There is one letter that, if added to each of the following four-letter words, will form three new five-letter words. What is the letter?

TANK   ACES   LATER

415. Complete the following analogy: Sister is to sibling as father is to _____.

Is the correct answer parent, mother, uncle, or brother?

416. At summer camp, three of the boys and three of the girls are challenged to find a way to get their group across the river in a two-person boat with the following condition: There can never be more boys than girls together. How can they get everyone across without violating the condition? Remember, the boat has to return with someone in it each time. (Hint: There are six round trips.)

417. By changing one letter in each of the words below, you can turn the words into two new words that are antonyms of each other. What are the two words you can create?

LEADER   FOSTER

418. Can you change the word HEAD to TOES in five steps by only changing one letter in the word at a time? Each change must create a real word. Since there is more than one way to solve it, make the ladder so the first change/ step is something you're doing right now, and the third step is a small amphibian that lives in ponds. There will be four words in between HEAD and TOES in this word ladder.

419. Can you think of a five-letter common Halloween costume which, when you remove a letter, becomes someone in charge of a party?

420. Luciana, Langston, Levi, Lincoln, and Lillian play on separate soccer teams. Their team names are the Bobcats, the Eagles, the Firebirds, the Pythons, and the Raptors. Each team has a different color jersey: blue, orange, yellow, purple, and red. Can you use the clues below to figure out what team each person is on and which color jersey they wear?

- Both Luciana's and Lincoln's jersey colors start with the same letter as their team names.

- Langston does not play for the Firebirds or the Pythons, but Lillian does.

- Levi plays for the Eagles and wears an orange jersey.

- Lincoln's jersey is the color combination of Luciana's and Lillian's jerseys.

- Levi's jersey is the color combination of Langston's and Lillian's jerseys.

421. Find words that rhyme with each of the words below. The first word is a category. The three words after that are words that fit within that category.

- The name of the category rhymes with FENCES.

- The words in the category rhyme with MUCH, KITE, and FELL.

What are the words?

422. Complete the following analogy: Breeze is to tornado as trickle is to _____.

Is the correct answer rain, earthquake, wind, or tidal wave?

423. If you change one letter in each of the words below, you can turn them into synonyms of one another. What are the three words? (Hint: It's not the same letter in each.)

START   CLOVER   BRAWNY

424. By changing one letter in each of the words below, you can turn the words into two new words that are antonyms of each other. What are the two words you can create?

PALS   MAIL

425. In one city, there are five different food trucks (tacos, pizza, gyros, salads, and hot dogs) on five different streets (Apple Ave., Badger Blvd., Charles Ct., Dominican Dr., and River Rd.). The five owners of the different food trucks are Ariel, Bailey, Cameron, Devon, and Riley. Each food truck serves a different number of items (4, 5, 6, 7, or 8). Using the clues below, can you figure out who owns which truck, where it is parked, and how many items they sell?

- Only the hot dog truck is parked on a street that starts with the same letter as its owner's name.

- Ariel does not sell tacos, hot dogs, or salads, but she does sell more items than anyone else besides Devon.

- Bailey sells gyros and sells fewer items than Cameron.

- The taco truck on Badger Blvd. is not owned by Devon.

- The salad truck sells the widest variety of items.

- The truck on Dominican Dr. does not sell gyros or hot dogs.

- The truck on River Rd. sells either gyros or salads and has fewer items than the hot dog truck.

- The pizza truck does not belong to Riley, who sells more items than Cameron but fewer than Devon.

7

YOUR TURN!

Congratulations on mastering all kinds of riddles! Are you ready to write some of your own? Coming up with riddles is just as much fun as solving them! If you have a friend or family member who enjoys riddles, too, make up riddles to try to stump each other. That way, you can create *and* solve riddles—the best of both worlds! It can be a little intimidating to come up with riddles from scratch, which is why I'm going to give you some guidelines and templates to make it easy to get started.

Write Your Own Riddles

Look for common objects in your home and make a list of each one's features. Choose some of those features that may have dual meanings or that are descriptive but won't give away the item too quickly.

> **Example:** Consider a pillow. It's white, soft, and fluffy. It's where you rest your head at night. It can be used as a weapon (*in a pillow fight*). It lives inside a case (*a pillowcase*).

Now think about something you enjoy and choose something about it to be your answer. Then brainstorm interesting ways to describe it that might stump someone.

> **Example:** If you like reading, your answer might be a bookmark. One tricky way to describe it would be to say that without it, you might lose track of where you are and have trouble finishing an adventure.

Practice being punny. Choose a topic and think of silly puns that fit it. Then, create a riddle that would lead someone to the punny solution.

> **Example:** Let's choose baked goods for our topic. Some puns related to it are: donut (*do not*) let me down, I had a filling (*feeling*) you would say that, and I whisk (*wish*) you wouldn't.

For an easy math riddle, write down a three-digit number. Then, make up clues that accurately describe the digits' relationships to one another.

> **Example:** Let's say we choose the number 471. We can say that the sum of the digits is 12, the first digit is even, the last digit is the smallest, and the middle digit is the greatest.

Sometimes there is more than one right answer to these kinds of riddles, so be prepared if someone comes up with an acceptably correct (or not wrong!) response. It might end up being pretty funny!

For logic puzzles, start with the names of three people. Then, select some characteristics they will each vary on. Decide which person will have which characteristics and construct clues that share enough details for someone to solve the riddle, without giving too much away. With these types of riddles, always be certain to try to solve your riddle using the clues you've provided to be sure you've included enough information to make the problem solvable.

> **Example:** Let's start with Aisha, Brian, and Kat. Each of them plays a different instrument and prefers a different style of music. We'll need to make sure to list all the instruments and musical styles and provide enough clues to cover all those options.

Create Your Own Clever Q&A Riddles

What has [*word that has two meanings*] but cannot [*verb that goes with the most common understanding of the feature*]?

> **Example:** What has [*legs*] but cannot [*walk*]?
>
> A table.

Create Your Own "What Am I?" Riddles

I am [*adjective*] and [*another adjective*]. People like [*feature that makes item likeable*]. You will not find me [*place you'd never find item*], but you may find me [*place you'd most likely find item*]. What am I?

> **Example:** I am round and flat. People like to have me for breakfast. You will not find me in the oven, but you might find me on the stove.
>
> (Answer: A pancake)

Create Your Own Puns

What did the [*noun*] say to the [*another noun*]?

> **Example:** What did the window say to the mirror?
>
> (Answer: "Hey, good looking.")

Create Your Own Brain Teasers

What do the following words have in common? [*List words you've chosen with something in common.*]

> **Example:** What do the following words have in common? Ball, thing, bummer, splinter. (*They rhyme with the four seasons: fall, spring, summer, winter.*)

Create Your Own Fun Math Riddles

By looking at the pattern below, can you determine which number comes next? [*Come up with a rule and generate numbers that fit it.*]

> **Example:** 1, 2, 4, 8, 16, ?
>
> > (Answer: 32. Each number doubles the preceding number.)

Create Your Own Logic Analogies

Complete the following analogy: [*adjective that describes noun*] is to [*noun described by adjective*] as [*adjective*] is to_____.

> **Example:** Red is to apple as yellow is to (*banana*).

Answer Key

Chapter 4: Brain Teasers

288. Sand.

289. "Each" is the name of one of her children. Only the child named Each took a cookie.

290. It can happen when the horse is running around a track! The legs closer to the outside of the track travel farther than the legs on the inner side of the track.

291. The president remains the president.

292. The four people are musicians who were hired to perform at an event.

293. The refrigerator door.

294. He's too short to reach the buttons for the higher floors.

295. Benjamin is telling the truth. Since we know that one of them must be from Fibster and the other one must be from Verity, Benjamin's statement is accurate.

296. Fill a cup or bowl with water and stand under it for longer than three minutes. Technically, you'll have stayed "underwater" for longer.

297. It's 17. Each number in the series has one more letter when spelled out than the previous number. Since 15 has eight letters, the next number must have nine letters: S-E-V-E-N-T-E-E-N.

298. First, place three sugar cubes on each side of the scale. If the scale balances, the seventh cube that wasn't weighed is the heavier one, and you don't need a second weighing. If one side is heavier than the other, set the three from the lighter side aside. For the second time using the scale, place one cube from the heavier side on one side of the scale, and a second cube on the other side of the scale. If the scale balances, the third cube from the original heavy side is the heavy cube. If the scale doesn't balance, the heavier cube will be alone on the heavy side.

299. NOTABLE: notable, no table, not able

300. The letter *e* doesn't appear in it, which is unusual since *e* is the most commonly used letter in the English language.

301. You should go to the one with the poor haircut, since they are the only other barber in town and must have given the fantastic haircut.

302. Wash saw.

303. If the sister is correct that her brother wrote "No" on both pieces, she should tear up the piece of paper she chooses without looking at it. They will then have to look at the other piece of paper she *didn't* choose. If it says "No," that means the torn-up pieces *should* have said "Yes." She will not only get the cookie, but outsmart her sneaky brother.

304. Johnathan is right and the parents aren't hiding any candy. If Katie's statement is correct then all statements are true, and only one statement is right. If Ellie's statement is correct, so is Katie's, which is impossible, as we know only one statement can be correct. Since Katie's statement cannot be correct, then Jonathan is right and the parents must be hiding *less* than one candy bar, which is zero.

305. By driving in reverse.

306. A cookie is $12. The bakery charges $2 per letter in the baked good's name.

307. Each of them can be turned into a new word by replacing the last letter of the word with the letter *n*.

308. They must be elected.

309. The first two people are from Verity and the third is from Fibster. Since people from Fibster always lie and people from Verity always tell the truth, when asked where they are from, both will always say they are from Verity. Thus, even though you didn't hear the first person's response, we know he must have said he was from Verity, so the second person was telling the truth.

310. The lake was frozen, so it was easy to walk across.

311. They are fake. No one referred to World War I by that name until World War II began. Since BCE and CE weren't used until the year 1582, it would be impossible to find authentic scrolls dated correctly before then (especially when no one prior to year 0 would know what they were counting down to!). Therefore, the items are worthless.

312. It's Ava. If the other two were telling the truth, the mess must have happened after Claire was in the kitchen, and Michael hadn't been in there all day. But the real clue is that Mrs. Yang didn't mention that the mess was a broken glass. Only the person who broke the glass would know what the mess was.

313. If you change the first letter of each word, you can turn them into directions: north, south, east, and west.

314. Pick up the second glass and pour the water into the fifth glass and return the now-empty glass to its original position.

315. Her brother.

316. Push the cork into the bottle and pour the gemstone out.

317. Club.

318. They were the same person: Grover Cleveland.

319. What time is it?

320. They are all palindromes (spelled the same backward and forward).

321. Being "mean."

322. U472BMT. You=U, force heaven = 47, to = 2, be = B, empty = MT.

323. Lucas. Each person's mode of transportation shares the same third letter with the person's name.

324. If you take away the first letter, the remaining letters are the same forward and backward.

325. He bought a candle and matches. He lit the candle and filled the room with light.

326. They were playing soccer, not baseball.

327. She is from Verity. No matter where the person behind her was from, he would have answered "Verity" (if he was from Verity, he'd tell the truth and say Verity, and if he was from Fibster, he'd lie and say Verity). If she was from Verity, she'd tell the truth and say that he said he was from Verity. If she was from Fibster, she'd lie and say he was from Fibster. Since we know his answer had to be Verity, that means she told the truth, which means she is from Verity.

328. C. "Fred is silly." The first letter of the word in each sentence spells out an animal (A = dog, B = cat, D = bird).

329. Ask him which path leads to his village. If he is from Verity, he will point you toward Verity since he will tell the truth. If he is from Fibster, he will also point you toward Verity since he will be dishonest.

330. All of them can be preceded by the word "water."

331. Ewe. Each word in the sequence begins with the last two letters of the word before it.

332. India (starting after the "w" in wind and ending before the "m" in am).

333. One. Just Zara, who was on her way to the market. Since the family members she met were carrying bags of food, they were walking the opposite direction on Main Street.

334. She slices the cake in half separating top from bottom.

BRAIN BENDER

335. Turn on the first two switches and leave them on for several minutes. Then, turn the first switch off. Go to the basement. The light that is on is the one that is controlled by the second switch. Feel the two bulbs that are off. The one that is warm is controlled by the first switch. (It will be warm from being on for several minutes before you turned it off.)

Chapter 5: Fun with Math

336. 55 + 5 = 60 (Tricky, right? Never said it had to be a set of three identical numbers!)

337. 574.

338. Nineteen: 8, 18, 28, 38, 48, 58, 68, 78, 80, 81, 82, 83, 84, 85, 86, 87, 88, 89, 98.

339. 462 + 357 = 819

340. 87. The numbers are upside down. If you turn them right side up, you'll see they count up from 86 to 91.

341. 12 days. It takes each painter two days to paint one room. Two days times six rooms equals 12 days total.

342. 1.5 miles. To solve this puzzle, use the formula 12x + 20x = 48 (12 minutes/mile times the distance to your friend's house plus 20 minutes/mile times the return distance in 48 total minutes.)

343. 48. If Sebastian's two snacks were one-fourth of what he had left, that means he must have had eight snacks. But before he ate those eight, remember they each ate half of the original snacks Sebastian brought. That means he would have had started with 16. Sixteen snacks times three friends is 48 total snacks. Verify the math this way: If each were given 16, each ate 8 at the start, leaving them with 8 each. Zain then ate one-fourth of his 8, or 2. Randall ate one-eighth of his, or 1. Sebastian ate three-fourths of his 8, or 6 (leaving two).

344. Six girls and three boys.

345. Mia will be 94 since she is six years younger than Miguel. (Many people think this is easy and answer too quickly, without thinking; many guess the answer is 50, incorrectly thinking she will still be half his age.)

346. Hot dogs are $2 each. Each water bottle costs $1.

347. Marion is 8 and Jamie is 5.

348. $A = 1, C = 2, D = 3, E = 7, G = 0, N = 4, O = 6, P = 5, T = 8$

349. Eleven. Adrien lost three times to Amari, so Adrien had lost $3 at some point in the game. Adrien would have to have won another three games to win back those $3, plus another five games to end up with $5 at the end.

350. 17. Each increase is one more than the one before (add one to the first number, add two to the second, three to the third . . .), so the fifth number will have five added to it, and the next number will be five more than 12: $1 + 2 = 3, 2 + 3 = 5, 3 + 5 = 8, 4 + 8 = 12, 5 + 12 = 17$.

351. $2 + 9 \times 3 - 1 \div 4 = 8$

352. He makes a profit of $4. He's initially out $5, so $-\$5 + \$7 = \$2$ profit. Then he pays 10 new dollars and sells for $12, earning a new $2 profit. $\$2 + \$2 = \$4$.

353. 119.

354. \$128. You could draw three of each denomination and finally draw a fourth \$20 bill. $3 \times 1 + 3 \times 5 + 3 \times 10 + 4 \times 20 = \$128$.

355. 4,236.

356. Nine years. Since it doubles in size every year, the year before it reaches its maximum height, it will be at half its maximum height.

357. 27. The eight that were left were two-thirds of what Alyssa left, so she must have left 12. Twelve was two-thirds of what Alex had left, meaning Tyler started with 18. Eighteen was two-thirds of what Alex found when he discovered the full bowl, and 18 is two-thirds of 27.

358. 1 and 9. $1 \times 9 = 9, 1 + 9 = 10$.

359. 1, 2, and 3. $1 + 2 + 3 = 6$ and $1 \times 2 \times 3 = 6$.

360. 18. Mr. Malik's back bumper, the front bumper of the 10th car, and the front and back bumpers of the eight cars between them.

361. 100. $\frac{9}{10}$ of $1000 = 900$, $\frac{8}{9}$ of $900 = 800$, $\frac{7}{8}$ of $800 = 700, \ldots, \frac{1}{2}$ of $200 = 100$.

362. Start by cooking the first side of burgers 1 and 2. After five minutes, flip over burger 1, set burger 2 aside, and begin cooking burger 3. After five more minutes, remove burger 1 (it's now fully cooked), flip burger 3, and return burger 2 to the grill to finish the uncooked side. In five more minutes, all three burgers will be fully cooked, and the total cook time is 15 minutes.

363. Just after 12. She must have arrived to hear the last chime from the 12 o'clock chimes. The next chime she heard was the half-hour chime at 12:30, and the final chime was the chime indicating one o'clock.

364. Harper is 14 and her mother is 41.

365. Three: he has one dog, one cat, and one bird.

366. Three. If you only pick up two socks, one might be white and the other gray. When you pick up a third sock, it will either be white or gray and match one of the first two socks you drew no matter what.

367. 10 cents. Most people will guess 20 cents, assuming the pencil costs $1, but since it costs $1 MORE than the eraser, that math doesn't work (i.e., if the eraser is 20 cents, the pencil would be $1.20 and together they would cost $1.40). Thus, the eraser is only 10 cents, the pencil is $1.10, and together they are $1.20.

368. E = 0, N = 3, O = 4, H = 5, T = 6, U = 7, F = 9

369. Two minutes. Each child will sharpen four pencils (12 pencils divided by three children). Each pencil takes 30 seconds to sharpen. Since each child has their own sharpener and thus can sharpen simultaneously, it will take them 30 seconds for each of their four pencils for a total of two minutes.

370. Kai collected five shark teeth and Carmen collected seven.

371. 200 feet. For every three feet Kabir moves forward, he is traveling 4 feet to make up for the backslide. Since the hill is 150 feet tall, he'll be making up 50 feet (150 feet divided by 3 feet equals 50, the number of times Kabir will backslide). Thus, Kabir will travel 150 feet plus an additional 50 feet to make up for the backslides every 3 feet.

372. Once the water starts boiling, she can start both the 3-minute timer and 10-minute timer. As soon as the 3-minute timer runs out, she can add the tea to the boiling water. The 10-minute timer will have seven minutes left at that point, so as soon as it runs out, her tea will be done.

373. 28. Each number in the sequence is the previous number plus the position of the current number. The last number is in the seventh position, so it is 21 + 7.

374. The first bag contains 22 pennies, the next bag contains 24, the third bag contains 26, and the fourth bag contains 28 pennies. 22 + 24 + 26 + 28 = 100 (The equation would look like this: $x + (x + 2) + (x + 4) + (x + 6) = 100$; solve for x).

375. More likely. You know you aren't holding the bag with two black marbles, so you're holding either the bag with two white marbles or the one with one white marble and one black marble. Out of three remaining marbles in those two bags, two are white. Therefore, you have a two-thirds chance of drawing a white marble, and a one-third chance that it will be black.

376. Yes, the rabbit will *just* make it to the hole in time. The rabbit will take 10 seconds to reach the hole (40 yards at 4 yards per second). Though the fox is moving faster, it will have to first make up the 10 yards between it and the rabbit. It will reach the rabbit's hole at the exact moment the rabbit does, 10 seconds into the chase (50 yards at 5 yards per second).

377. A = 2, B = 1, C = 3. This problem is easier than it appears. Since there are only three digits, we can determine 1, 2, and 3 simply by looking at the first letter in each of the numbers (representing the thousands position). B < A < C, which means C must be the largest digit (3) and B must be the smallest (1).

378. It takes five days. On day one she places 162 cards, on day two she adds 108 more cards (total cards placed = 270), on day three she adds 72 more cards (total = 342), on day four she added 48 more (total = 390), and on day five she adds the remaining 26 cards (total = 416). For pure math, two-thirds of 48 would have been 32, but at that point she only had 26 cards remaining.

379. 4,632.

380. $4 \times 3 \div 6 + 8 - 1 = 9$

381. $2.50. Together they spent $7 so each should pay $3.50. Omar has already paid $1 so just owes the difference ($3.50 − $1 = $2.50).

382. 18. For each set of numbers, the second number is subtracted from the first number and then doubled to calculate the third number $(4 - 3 = 1, 1 \times 2 = 2; 10 - 6 = 4, 4 \times 2 = 8; 15 - 7 = 8, 8 \times 2 = 16; 7 - 5 = 2, 2 \times 2 = 4; 8 - 1 = 7, 7 \times 2 = 14; 12 - 3 = 9, 9 \times 2 = 18)$.

BRAIN BENDER

383. Emery will always out-earn Theo. During the first three months, Theo will make $5 + $6 + $7 = $18. Emery will make $2.50 + $2.75 + $3.00 + $3.25 + $3.50 + $3.75 = $18.75. Continuing for the rest of the year, Theo will make $18 (from the first three months) + $8 + $9 + $10 + $11 + $12 + $13 + $14 + $15 + $16 = $126. Emery will earn $18.75 + $4.00 + $4.25 + $4.50 + $4.75 + $5.00 + $5.25 + $5.50 + $5.75 + $6.00 + $6.25 + $6.50 + $6.75 + $7.00 + $7.25 + $7.50 + $7.75 + $8.00 + $8.25 = $129.

Chapter 6: Logic Puzzles

384. TALK → TASK

385. Samir prefers math, Kendall prefers reading, Harley prefers music, Eden prefers science, and Drew prefers social studies. We know Harley and Drew's favorites from clues 2 and 4, which leaves math, reading, and science for the remaining friends. Eden likes math or science, but since neither Samir nor Kendall likes science, Eden's favorite must be science. Since Samir dislikes reading, math is the only possibility left as her favorite, leaving Kendall with reading.

386. The letter *E*: cheat, below, reset.

387. Finger. A scarf is something you wear around your neck. A ring is something you wear on your finger.

388. Paris plays soccer, Raven plays baseball, and Corey plays basketball.

389. Tuesday.

390. Mila, Lulu, Dani, Owen, Elijah.

391. The person from Kenya (who lives in the blue house) owns the fish.

392. First, he must take the rabbit across and return alone. Next, he brings the lettuce across. He leaves the lettuce on that side of the river but returns with the rabbit. Once back, he swaps the rabbit for the dog and brings the dog across. Then, he returns alone to fetch the rabbit.

393. Three students were wearing solid colored shirts. No students were wearing solid red shirts ($12 - 8 - 3 - 1 = 0$). One student was wearing a solid blue shirt ($10 - 8 - 1 = 1$). Two students were wearing solid yellow shirts ($6 - 3 - 1 = 2$). Zero solid red shirts plus 1 solid blue shirt plus 2 solid yellow shirts equals 3 solid colored shirts.

394. No. Since all peanut-filled candies are red, and Jules does not like red candies but does like all the candies in the bowl, there must not be any red candies in the bowl; thus, there are no candies with peanuts inside in the bowl.

395. The category is NUMBER and the words are EIGHT, NINE, and TEN.

396. Joyce's favorite color is blue and she likes oranges best. Ruby's favorite color is green (the only one that is a blend of two colors), and she prefers bananas. Isaac's favorite color is yellow and his favorite fruit is kiwi. (We know because yellow and blue are the only colors that mix to make Ruby's green. His fruit can't be yellow, so it has to be kiwi.) Camilla's favorite color is red, and she loves cherries. (They match colors.)

397. PLANE → PLANT

398. Orchard. An acorn grows into a tree, which is part of a forest, just as a seed grows into a fruit tree, which is part of an orchard.

399. The letter *G*: rugby, thing, surge.

400. Yard and beak.

401. Chloe and Amit cross first in two minutes. Then Chloe returns alone in one minute. Next, Maliah and Oliver cross together in eight minutes. Amit returns with the flashlight to retrieve Chloe, taking two minutes each way. $2+1+8+2+2=15$.

402. Moisture. If someone is hungry, they lack food. If something is dry, it lacks moisture.

403. Remove an item from the "PENCILS & ERASERS" bin. If it's a pencil, that bin should be labeled "PENCILS" since we know that the "PENCILS & ERASERS" is incorrect and yet the bin contains pencils. The bin labeled "PENCILS" should be labeled "ERASERS" because if it contains pencils and erasers then the third bin would be labeled "ERASERS" and contain erasers, which isn't possible since we know *all* three bins are mislabeled. Thus, the first bin should be "PENCILS," the second bin "ERASERS," and the third bin "PENCILS & ERASERS." Similarly, if the first item you draw from the "PENCILS & ERASERS" bin is an eraser instead of a pencil, then it should be labeled "ERASERS," the bin labeled "ERASERS" should be labeled "PENCILS," and the bin labeled "PENCILS" should be labeled "PENCILS & ERASERS."

404. The two children must go across first. One child gets out, and the other returns. Upon returning, the child gets out and one of the parents crosses to the other side. Once there, the parent gets out and the child comes back in the boat to pick up the other child, and they return to the far side. One child gets out to wait with the parent while the other child crosses back to the start. The other parent now goes across, and the child there brings the boat back to pick up the other child; they both cross to the far side together. Although the family is together, they must still return the boat to the fisherman on the other side so one child comes back, gets out, and lets the fisherman cross. Once across, the fisherman gets out, the child gets in and returns to pick up the other child. They return to the far side where the fisherman gets in his boat to go on his way, while the family continues their backpacking adventure.

405. Deep and shallow.

406. COOL → POOL

407. WARM → WARD → CARD → CORD → COLD

408. Stir and teen.

409. Sweep. A pencil is used to write. A broom is used to sweep.

410. Dominique is turning 5 and getting a video game, Aidan is turning 10 and getting a bike. Yuki is turning 8 and getting a puppy. Zara is turning 12 and getting clothes.

411. The category is DRINK and the words are MILK, WATER, and JUICE.

412. Soda and lily.

413. Violet was wearing a magenta dress, Magenta was wearing a rose dress, and Rose was wearing a violet dress. We know Violet was wearing magenta because she couldn't be wearing violet (none of the girls' dresses matched their names), and we know she wasn't wearing rose because the girl wearing the rose-colored dress answered her.

414. The letter *H*: thank, aches, lather.

415. Parent. A sister is, by definition, a sibling. A father is, by definition, a parent.

416. First, one boy and one girl must cross, and the girl must return with the boat. Then, two boys can cross, with one boy making the return trip. Next, two girls will cross, and a boy and a girl return. Now, two girls cross, and one boy returns. He goes back and forth twice to pick up each remaining boy.

417. Header and footer.

418. HEAD → READ → ROAD → TOAD → TOED → TOES

419. GHOST → HOST

420. Luciana = blue Bobcats, Langston = yellow Raptors, Levi = orange Eagles, Lincoln = purple Pythons, Lillian = red Firebirds. We know from the third clue that Levi's jersey is orange and that he plays for the Eagles. The fourth clue reveals that Langston and Lillian's jerseys must be red and yellow. The only other colors that can combine to create one of the listed jersey colors are red and blue to make purple. We already know Lillian's color must be red or yellow, so it can't be blue, and thus must be red, meaning that Luciana's jersey must be blue. From the first clue, we know Luciana's team name starts with the same letter as her jersey color, so Luciana's team must be the Bobcats. Since Lillian's jersey is red, Langston's jersey must be yellow. Following the color combination logic, we know Lincoln's jersey must be purple (red + blue) and from the first clue, we know his team must be the Pythons. That leaves just the Firebirds and the Raptors for Langston and Lillian. From the second clue, we know Langston is not on the Firebirds, and thus must be a Raptor, meaning Lillian must be a Firebird.

421. The category is SENSES and the words are TOUCH, SIGHT, and SMELL.

422. Tidal wave. Breeze is a light wind, while a tornado is a devastating wind. A trickle is a small flow of water, while a tidal wave is a devastating flow of water.

423. Smart, clever, and brainy.

424. Pass and fail.

425. Ariel owns the pizza truck on Dominican Dr. that sells 7 items. Bailey owns the gyros truck on River Rd. that sells 4 items. Cameron owns the hot dog truck on Charles Ct. that sells 5 items. Devon owns the salad truck on Apple Ave. that sells 8 items. And Riley owns the taco truck on Badger Blvd. that sells 6 items.

We know from the second clue that Ariel must sell pizza or gyros. Since we know from the third clue that Bailey sells gyros, Ariel must sell pizza. We also know from the second clue that Ariel sells 7 items and Devon sells 8. We know from the fifth clue that Devon must sell salads, meaning Cameron and Riley must sell hot dogs and tacos, though we don't know who sells which yet. From the eighth clue, we know that Riley sells more than Cameron, and from the third clue we know Bailey sells less than Cameron, so Bailey must sell only 4 items, Cameron must sell 5, and Riley must sell 6. From the seventh clue, we know that the truck on River Rd. must be Bailey's gyros. The first clue rules out the possibility of Riley selling hot dogs, meaning Cameron must sell them and is parked on Charles Ct. Riley must sell tacos, and we know from the fourth clue that the taco truck is on Badger Blvd. Again from the first clue, we know that Ariel can't be parked on Apple Ave., so that must be where Devon's truck is, leaving Dominican Dr. as the only possibility for Ariel's truck. We know from the seventh clue that the truck on River Rd. must sell gyros. It can't be Devon's salads since it sells fewer items than the hot dog truck. Thus, Bailey owns the truck on River Rd.

From the last clue, we know the pizza truck must belong to Cameron, and Riley must sell hot dogs. From the first clue, we know that Riley's truck is parked on River Rd.

About the Author

CORINNE SCHMITT is the author of *Super Fun Family Card Games* and the blogger behind *Wondermom Wannabe*. She is an avid fan of riddles, puzzles, and brain teasers. Corinne graduated from the University of Illinois with a degree in English literature and a master's in business administration. She is married to a retired US Marine and has five children, all of whom share her love of riddles. She currently resides in Northern Virginia.

About the Illustrator

DYLAN GOLDBERGER is an illustrator and printmaker based in Brooklyn, New York. He grew up in New Rochelle and moved to Brooklyn in 2007 to attend Pratt Institute, graduating with a BFA in communication design. His self-published alphabet book, *See Spot Shred*, released in 2015, reveals his love of dogs and skateboarding, recurring themes throughout his artwork. When he's not working in the studio, he's out exploring the parks and streets of New York City with his dog Townes. His illustrations have been used by many notable brands and publications.